Carol
OF THE
Brown
King

For my friends
Barbara Pringle and Darwin Henderson
Look there at the Star!
—A.B.

Carol
OF THE
Brown
King

Nativity Poems by **Langston Hughes**

illustrated by **Ashley Bryan**

◆

a jean karl book
atheneum books for young readers

Carol of the Brown King

Of the three Wise Men
Who came to the King,
One was a brown man,
So they sing.

Of the three Wise Men
Who followed the Star,
One was a brown king
From afar.

They brought fine gifts
Of spices and gold
In jeweled boxes
Of beauty untold.

Unto His humble
Manger they came
And bowed their heads
In Jesus' name.

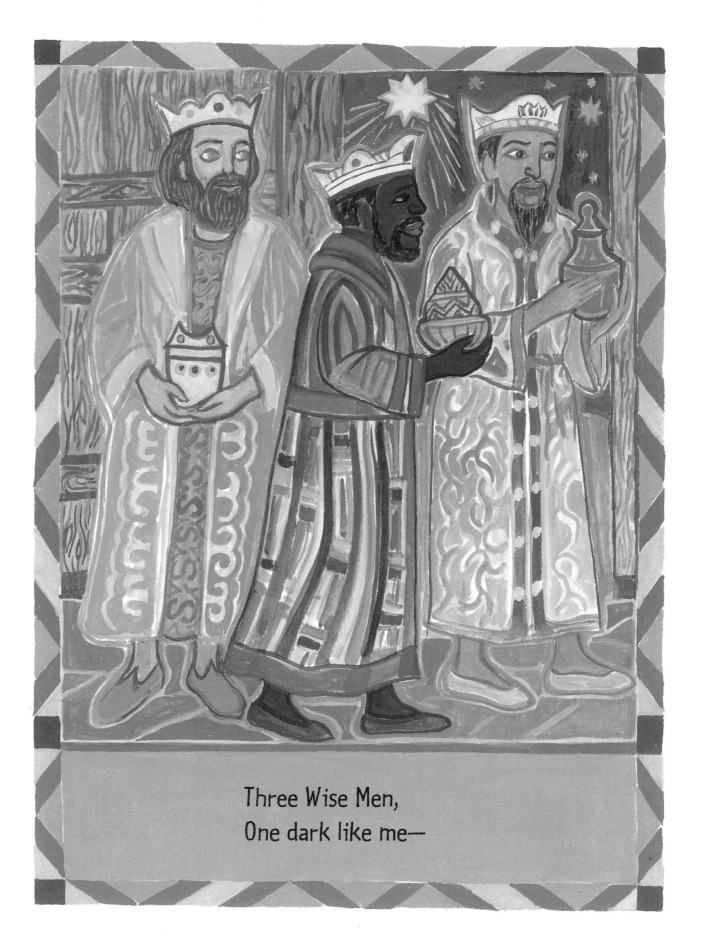

Three Wise Men,
One dark like me—

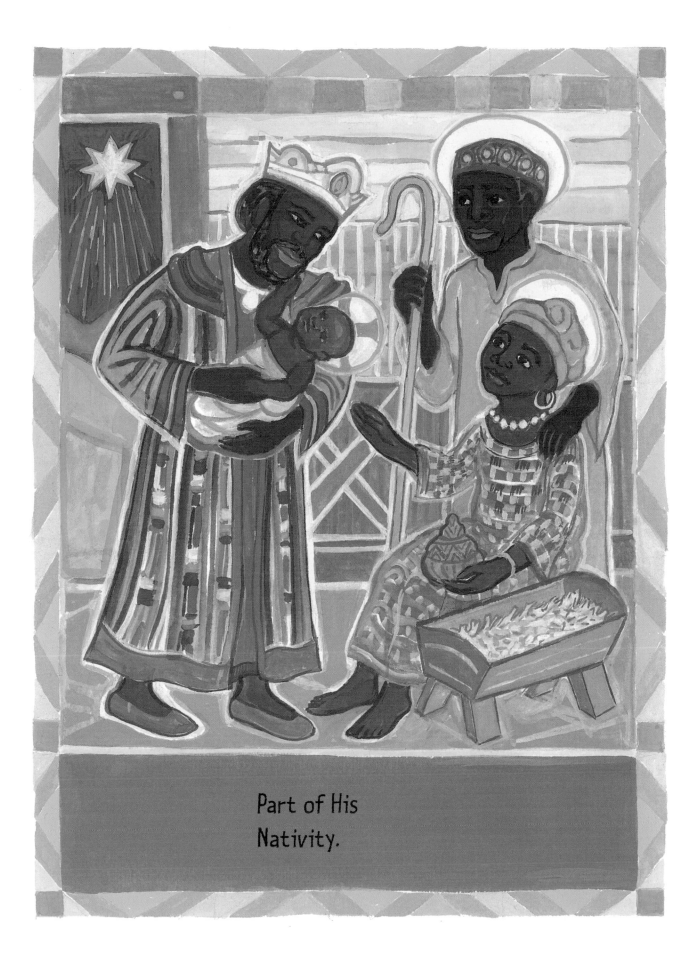

Part of His
Nativity.

Shepherd's Song at Christmas

Look there at the star!
I, among the least,
Will arise and take
A journey to the East.
But what shall I bring
As a present for the King?
What shall I bring to the Manger?

I will bring a song,
A song that I will sing,
A song for the King
In the Manger.

Watch out for my flocks,
Do not let them stray.
I am going on a journey
Far, far away.
But what shall I bring
As a present for the Child?
What shall I bring to the Manger?

I will bring a lamb.
Gentle, meek, and mild,
A lamb for the Child
In the Manger.

I'm just a shepherd boy,
Very poor I am—
But I know there is
A King in Bethlehem.
What shall I bring
As a present just for Him?
What shall I bring to the Manger?

I will bring my heart
And give my heart to Him.
I will give my heart
To the Manger.

On a Christmas Night

In Bethlehem on a Christmas night
All around the Child shone a holy light.
All around His head was a halo bright
On a Christmas night.

"We have no room," the innkeeper called,
So the glory fell where the cows were stalled,
But among the guests were Three Kings who called
On a Christmas night.

How can it be such a light shines here
In this humble stable once cold and drear?
Oh, the Child has come to bring good cheer
On a Christmas night!

And what is the name of the little One?
His name is Jesus—He's God's own Son.
Be happy, happy, everyone
On a Christmas night!

On a Pallet of Straw

They did not travel in an airplane,
They did not travel by car,
They did not travel on a streamline train.
They traveled on foot from afar,
They traveled on foot from afar.

They did not seek for a fine hotel,
They did not seek an inn,
They did not seek a bright motel.
They sought a cattle bin,
They sought a cattle bin.

Who were these travelers on the road?
And where were they going? And why?
They were Three Wise Men who came from the East,
And they followed a star in the sky,
A star in the sky.

What did they find when they got to the barn?
What did they find near the stall?
What did they find on a pallet of straw?
They found there the Lord of all!
They found the Lord of all!

An Anonymous Verse
translated from a Puerto Rican Christmas card

Lady Santa Ana
Why does the Child cry?

About an orange He's lost
and cannot spy.

Tell Him not to cry
For I have two—

One for the Child
And one for you.

The Christmas Story

Tell again the Christmas story:
Christ is born in all His glory!
Baby laid in manger, dark
Lighting centuries with the spark
Of innocence that is the Child
Trusting all within His smile.

Tell again the Christmas story
With the halo of His glory:
Halo born of humbleness
By the breath of cattle blest,
By the poverty of stall
Where a bed of straw is all,

By a door closed at the inn
Where only men of means get in,
By a door closed to the poor
Christ is born on earthen floor
In a stable with no lock—

Yet kingdoms tremble at the shock
Of infant King in swaddling clothes
At an address no one knows
Because there is no painted sign—
Nothing but a star divine,

Nothing but a halo bright
About His young head in the night,
Nothing but the wondrous light
Of innocence that is the Child
Trusting all within His smile.

Mary's Son of golden star:
Wise Men journey from afar!

Mary's Son in manger born:
Music of an Angel's horn!

Mary's Son in straw and glory:
Wonder of the Christmas story!

Atheneum Books for Young Readers
An imprint of Simon & Schuster Children's Publishing Division
1230 Avenue of the Americas
New York, New York 10020

"Carol of the Brown King," "Shepherd's Song at Christmas," "On a Christmas Night,"
"On a Pallet of Straw," "The Christmas Story," from
COLLECTED POEMS by Langston Hughes.
Copyright © 1994 by the Estate of Langston Hughes. Reprinted by permission of Alfred A. Knopf, Inc.

Illustrations copyright © 1998 by Ashley Bryan

Book design by Ann Bobco
The text of this book is set in Kosmik-Plain One
The illustrations are rendered in tempera and gouache paintings

First Edition

Printed in the United States of America

10 9 8 7 6 5 4 3 2 1

Library of Congress Cataloging-in-Publication Data:
Hughes, Langston, 1902–1967.
Carol of the brown king: nativity poems by Langston Hughes; illustrated by Ashley Bryan.
p.   cm.
Summary: Five poems by Langston Hughes and one anonymous one translated from the Spanish
present the story of the first Christmas from different perspectives.
ISBN 0-689-81877-7
1. Christmas—Juvenile poetry. 2. Children's poetry, American.
[1. Jesus Christ—Nativity—Poetry. 2. Christmas—Poetry. 3. American poetry—Collections.] I. Bryan, Ashley, ill. II. Title.
PS3515.U274C37   1998
811'.52—dc21
97-30814   CIP   AC

FIRST
EDITION